bing bong!

ATTENTION, PASSENGERS:
WELCOME TO
Trebleopolis!

HAPPY BIRTHDAY

Finally!

I'm **SO** ready to get off this train!

Now, now, Almond! Let's be sure not to forget anything.

You have the Dream Sword, right?

You know it!

Great! Then let's go.

how

3

Huh? My birthday was—

Not **you**, silly!

It's our city's biggest birthday bash...

... and everyone's invited!

Even tourists!

Especially tourists!

Wow, how exciting!

So whose birthday is it?

You **really** don't know?

The center of this jubilee...

... is our biggest V. I. P....

... the one who makes us say

"ooh-weeeeee"...

can i please go home

Huh?

Oh! Princess Nautilus!

Here for the party?

Did you bring presents?!

Were we supposed to?

Hail and happy birthday, Queen Cymbal!

We're actually here on urgent business.

Your Majesties, one of the Nightmare Knight's underlings is lurking in the Melody kingdom at this very moment.

We think Princess Piano is in danger!

Wha? I don't know about any underlings.

As for Piano, she's in her room getting ready for the concert tonight.

Concert?!

Wow! I haven't heard her perform in years!

You're in for a treat!

Uhhh...

We're sorry. She'll be very happy to see you...

...but that's why.

My Piano's calm enough most of the time...

but give her any reason to start hollering, and she can't control herself!

When she's worked up, she yells so loud, the **SPACE** Kingdom can hear her!

It's crazy!

I dunno where she GETS IT FROM!!!

I don't either, dear.

tap
tap.

from a
fan.

We're really gonna sit here and listen to music for an **hour?!**

The program says 110 minutes.

Seriously?!

That's—that's, like, **MORE** than an hour!

Almond, it is essential for Dreamside's youth to develop an appreciation for the arts. Why, one day, when you're older, you'll reflect on this experience and think—

N-Now, see here!

I'll wake you up when it's over if you want.

I knew I could count on you.

Oh, my poor PIAAANO! I can't BEARRR it!!

Hey, don't worry! Saving princesses is kinda our job.

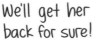

We'll get her back for sure!

And we'll do whatever it takes to protect this city from Noisemaster!

Your Majesties, where is this "Rhythm Ridge" he spoke of?

Hm...

That would be on the other side of the wall...

Which means there's only one way to get there!

Noisemaster, come forth.

Well, well, WELL!

Check it: my boy and me? **MAD SCHEMIN'** up in here!

We got a plan so **ILL,** it'll put you in a **HOSPITAL!**

Noisemaster.

For real, though.

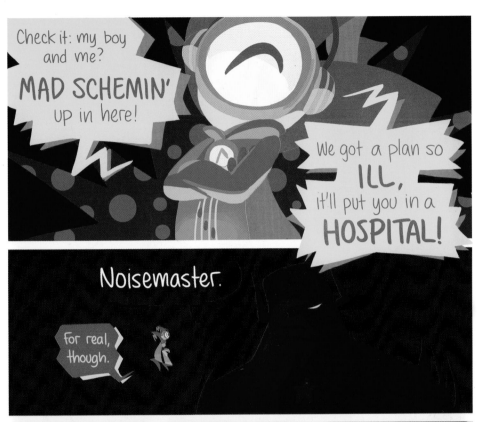

... I suppose you **have** managed to capture the princess.

Very well.

And what of the legendary hero?

Comin' at ya, Big Man!

Eventually, the two old boys got so loud, it was scary.

The Oracle could hear the noise up in her sanctuary.

"This just won't do!" she said.

"I'll end this war once and for all!"

One thing could put the feud to bed...

... a giant, soundproof wall!

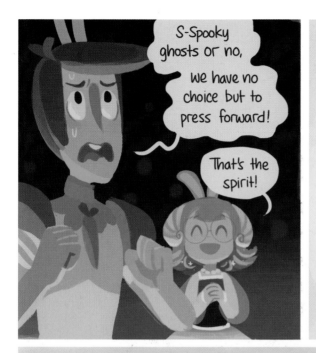

S-Spooky ghosts or no, we have no choice but to press forward!

That's the spirit!

And I love spirit! Now hold on tight, because we're going...

... down?

W-What?! Why are we going DOWN?

HUH?!

Is he gone?

Is he gone?!

He's been gone for, like, two hours.

You're totally freaking.

I KNOW! And it's **frying me up!!**

I can't believe that Nightmare Nimrod—

you said he was gone, right—

humiliated me in front of the princess like that! And now he's got me too spooked to do my job right!

Like, get a grip! You're way cooler than this, y'know?

Yeah! And, I mean, the princess hated you anyway, so who needs her!

Can it, you!

If you weren't such a complete **SCREW-UP**, I wouldn't be **IN** this mess!

Huh?!

B-But, sir, **you** were the one who took her necklace! I just—

CAN IT, I SAID!!

You're **ALWAYS** ruining my chances with Parfait! Why do I even—

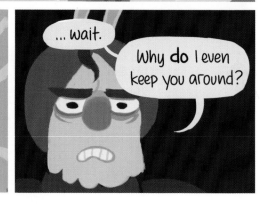

... wait.

Why **do** I even keep you around?

W-**Wha?** You can't really mean that, sir!

Oh, I **MEAN** it, all right!

You've gotten in my way for the last time, you greasy good-for-nothing!

tweet

tweet

Sir Tomato... He's picked on me ever since the day we met...

...but I never thought he'd do something so mean...

siiigh

CRASH

Listen, that crash was pretty rough—you sure you're okay?

I guess...

...except we're **STILL ON THE WRONG SIDE!**

What do we do now?!

Crossing over, huh? Jeez, y'know, I wish I could help...

but unless you've got the Oracle's key, my lock won't budge an inch.

Key?

See, Her Dreamship built me to keep those old kings from fighting, right?

But she ALSO made that key in case they, like, changed their minds or whatever.

You know.

How **wise!**
She really **can** see the future!

Look, I know it's a pain, but it really is the ONLY way to unlock my door.

If you want to pass, you're gonna have to get a move on.

This can't be happening...!

Hey, no use crying about it!

If anybody can beat up monsters in record time, it's me!

And if anyone can complete mundane tasks in record time, it is me!

You two hold the fort! Let's do it, Carrothead!

Yes!

Rock it, guys!

Ohhhhhh!

Behold the power of positive thinking!

It must have scared him off.

I kind of doubt that.

Huff Huff

Hey!

We heard something—

WHOA!

The wall!

The guy!

The what?

uuuuuuuggggghhh

MEZZO!!

Mezzo, noooo!

How could we let this happen?!

cough, hack!!
D-Don't sweat it! I can take a hit or two.

But, hey, I guess this means you're golden!

Go wherever you want.

Just, uh...
If you see the Oracle, maybe tell her to come patch me up later?

S-Sure.

What a bummer!

I was kinda getting into that, y'know?

Nothing like a good errand to get one's blood going, eh?

But... how did Mezzo collapse like that?

Cuco?

W—

would you believe me if i said the nightmare knight let us through

49

All right,

I don't know where you came from or what you want here,

but you're going back.

NOW.

Oh!

I-I say!

Hey! What gives?!

Look, I'm sorry, but if you don't leave...

...It's too late. Just come to my house— I'll explain there.

Hurry!

Creeeeak

shut

Now.

Do you all know where you are?

Er... not precisely.

Is Rhythm Ridge nearby? Because that's where we—

It'll have to wait.

This is Organetto, and I'm Lute, the mayor.

We've got a problem on our hands, and until it's dealt with, I can't let you out after curfew.

Problem, huh?

What's up?

An ancient evil has...

... Well, I'll spare you the details.

To make a long story short —

No!

NOOOO NO NO NO NO NO NO NOOO

Miss Lute, **please** — you are the **mayor** of a **village**!

Is this **really** how you're going to tell adventuring heroes an ancient legend?

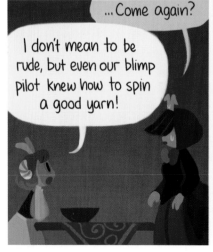

...Come again?

I don't mean to be rude, but even our blimp pilot knew how to spin a good yarn!

The poem was quite nice.

uh

um

I liked the pictures.

um

uhh

um

I-It's okay; you really don't have to—

ahem!

There once was a man named Legato.

A good sorcerer he was not...o.

A hero came by,

and defeated the guy...

S—

Something, something, "Legato"

aaaaaaaa.aa

tsk tsk

Oh, cut me some slack!

I'm a **mayor**, not a poet!

SMASH!

Listen, Count Legato terrorized our village over a century ago...

...and now he's back, doing it again!

Every night, he appears in the town square...

...and anyone unlucky enough to be there vanishes without a trace.

They—

...they don't come back.

H-How very frightening!

So... that's why there's a curfew?

Right.

I'm sorry to hold you up like this, but I can't let anyone else be made a victim.

AHA HA HA! Can't you?!

No!

hehe

Oh! Gee, I'm sorry.

I just got to this town, but nobody was around, so I got lonely...

...but then I heard someone laughing, and I thought I'd come see what was so funny!

...Oh, but this doesn't look funny.

sniff

sob

In fact, you look kinda like a mean guy.

You know, I **know** this really mean guy wh—

snap!

POOF!

Now! There is only one thing I lack!

If I cannot win the heart of Lady Concertina, all the world's adoration means **nothing!**

Uh, go to her, my prince.

I shall.

Greetings to the second-loveliest creature I've ever laid eyes on!

?

...

..."Prince"...

OH!

Prince Crescendo! I have found myself helplessly in love with you all of a sudden! Please marry me at your earliest convenience!

HAAAAAAA
HAHAHAHA!

BACON?!

It's been **so** long,
my darling prince!

And he's
pretty good?

Didn't you
miss me?!

This little thing, huh?

WHOA!

No touching unless you want an encore, kid!

That's... Huh?
A contact lens turned him into Legato?

Look, the count was... eccentric.

He made that so his magic wouldn't die with him.

Guess we should have hid it better, huh?

Geez, dude, I'm **SORRY**.

If I knew you were so sensitive—

I didn't raise a bully,

and I **know** I didn't raise a bully who can't **apologize**.

AGAGAGAGA

See, Mute, he can't handle all that screamin'.

When Piano went off, tch... that was it.

He was OUT.

Out, like... **knocked** out?

Yeah, it's real bad.

But if he hates screaming so much, why does he hang out with **you?**

...You don't get it, huh?

According to my studies, Noisemaster and Mutemaster were created at the same time,

so they share a very unique bond.

Couldn't you have remembered all of this a little bit soonevermindnevermindnevermindnevermindneve

Cucumber?

Sir Carr

W—What?

Hey, Princess.

All alone?

Princess! What's happened? Are you hurt?

Everything's fine.

heh heh

ha ha ha ha

HA HA HA HA

Oh no...

What...

...was **THAT?!**

Have we won?

I-I don't know...

It doesn't really feel like it.

G-
G-

Greetings, Hero!

Congratulations on defeating Noisemaster and, um... th-the other one!

Uh...are you okay?

Sweetie, after what just happened,

I think I've got good reason to be a bit **on edge.**

I don't remember how long it's been since I've had a scare like that.

But that barrier!

Of course!

It must have been **your** doing, right?

144

W-Well, I didn't want to come in BOASTING...

...but I suppose the secret's out.

Yes, that was me.

Wowww!

That's amazing, Your Dreamship!

I didn't even see you **do** anything!

If you could have stopped the Blaster **yourself,**

why did we even—

Listen, HERO—it's my job to **guide you**, not to do the hard parts for you.

Perhaps you shouldn't have taken so long to get here, hm?

BUT—

End of discussion.

...

Do I look like I'm in the mood?

W-We've all been through a lot...

Please try to understand.

Now, if that wraps up the **interrogation**, I'd like to get this part over with.

Disaster Stones, proof of your bravery, et cetera.

Just take them.

H-Hey, c'mon.

Chapter 2

Good Job!

At the last second, the terrible Noise Blaster was thwarted, saving Trebleopolis.

But what's this uneasy feeling hanging in the

Yes, yes, how nice for you.

Now, let's head back to Trebleopolis and discuss your next move.

Gather round!

We need a new member.

I dunno, like...

I think it's okay with just us—

It's not **WORKING,** Lettuce!

Sure, I know I'm both cool **and** manly enough to make my **own** entrance,

but losing a sidekick's really throwing my balance off, y'know?

Well, maybe you should have **thought** about that before you went totally nutso on Bacon or, like, whatever??

HEEEEEEELP!!

HEEEEELP!!

HEEEEI

Sheesh, Princess!

I love you and everything, but if you don't put a royal **sock in it,** the big guy's gonna think **I'M** making you cry!

S...
Sir Tomato...

Thank goodness!

Whoa, **WHAT?!**

Oh, Sir Tomato, c'est terrible...

Flattery'll getcha everywhere, Highness! What's the matter?

Well, just now, I was on the balcony, crying...

...or whatever you think I do...

I need a big, strong man to 'elp me with my problems.

And when I came back inside, my necklace...

Quelle horreur...!

It must 'ave fallen into le jardin...

It had such a weak chain...

Uh... that's too bad, Princess.

So what'd you call ME for?

Tomato! Are you really so cold?!

Look, I'm sorry, but I believe the phrase is "say fromage."

Like, "c'est dommage."

Yeah.

...Wait, huh?

Good evening, Princess.

I had hoped for a more creative escape plan from you.

P-Please...

Your room,
Princess.

creeelleeeaaak

Do not attempt
this again.

Oui, d'accord...

...

But—
wait.

P-Please.

I—

Being locked away
like this every day,
with no one but
Tomato to talk to...

I've never felt
more alone.

I understand if
you won't let
me go,

but...

Will you at
least stay and
listen to me?

Just for a
few minutes?

Make this brief.

Merci beaucoup!

I am always worrying, Sir Nightmare.

Worrying about my kingdom, about my papa...

...and about Sir Carrot.

The famous coward.

Ah, you've 'eard of him.

I-I mean, NO!

...

Oui, maybe he is not so brave.

But I know he's doing his best for me...

I miss him so much.

Sigh.

Désolée, Sir Nightmare.

I should not 'ave kept you like this.

But... thank you for listening.

For the first time in so long...

I'm glad I could make a new friend.

Mon cher Carrot,

My letters to you never seem to turn out right. Sometimes I see you reading the mushy things I write, and I get embarrassed... Other times, I imagine you worrying about me, and then I just end up crying.

This letter is already mushy, and I am already crying, so I guess I have nothing else to be afraid of! 🐰

Do you remember the night that shooting star fell onto my balcony? He said the pendants he gave us would keep us together even when we were far apart. I thought it was a little silly at the time, but I still wear mine every day.

I know you — you just reached for yours, didn't you? :🐰:

In truth, I know that you will probably never read this letter... But if some miracle really has brought it to your hands, there is something I want you to know...

...

AAAAAAAAAA!!!!

Peridot?!

What's wrong?
Are you hurt?!

I WENT TO THE MELOD
KINGDOM AND I LOOKE
REALLY CUTE AND I HAD
A GOOD ONE-LINER AN
HER SWORD WAS FAKE
AND I COULD'VE BEAT
HER   ED U
MES   SED
I MESSED UP I MESS
MESSED UP I MESSED
SSED UP I MESSED UP
MESSED UP I MESSED
I MESSED UP I MESS
MESSED UP I MESSED
SSED UP I MESSED UP
MES
I ME

Shh, darling.
It's all right.

We'll get them
next time.

We will?

Would I lie to my
favorite minion?

Come on—we'll
watch some more of
your show together.

Would you
like that?

Yeah!

You want my name on a **sword?**

Look, it's a long story.

Well, I've autographed weirder things...

Nautilus Plan

And this is the least I can do to thank you.

Cool!

Five kingdoms to go!

Um...

That includes the Crystal Kingdom... right?

Of course! Why do you ask?

Whenever you meet Ammie —

Uh— Princess Ametrine...

Can you give this to her for me?

I just, y'know...

p

...want to make sure she gets it.

It shall be delivered safely, Your Highness.

Thank y...

Wait a sec— it's **YOU!**

Parfait's boyfriend!

Yeah, I knew it!

How is she? Have you rescued her yet?

I'm

afraid not, Your Highness.

Sheesh! You're gonna be her ex-boyfriend if you don't hurry!

HA! HA! HA!

Anyway, good luck on your journey!

Come visit sometime, okay?

Sure!

I'm kidding.

Welcome aboard, honorary champions!

Now that my ship has been refueled,

your "Flow-er King-dom" should be only a few short minutes away!

Whoa, cool!

But...you're still headed for Caketown, right?

Isn't this a little out of the way for you?

Crazy talk, Cucumber!

This is the least I can do for a fellow ally of justice!

or a test subject.

Oho! Well, we ARE certainly—

180

W...

What did he mean by that?

Look!

Is...

that...

WARNING!

...the SUN?!

We're heading right into it!

We've got to turn back!

But the controls aren't responding!

So, what? We're just gonna **CRASH**, then?!

What else can we do?!

[200 SECONDS TO IMPACT.]

Ohh! This is the end, children!

Everyone, please **CALM DOWN!!**

ahem

Yes, I know we're all in the mood for getting out of this mess with our lives.

...What?

But there's one thing NOBODY'S in the mood forrrr...!!

No.

Yawwwwn...

Wowie-wow!

Another sunshiny, funshiny day!

You're the best pilot in the whooooooole dreamy world, Princess.

Thanks, pal!

You know I do my best.

Oh, but golly-wolly-osh!

Should I be worried about the pointy lil' saucer that's a-flyin' on over?

Uhh...

Listen, I know it's been a long day, but —

THAT'S A THING

• Expertly done,
Legendary Heroes.

• But I expected no less.

To be continued in...

The Flower Kingdom

Peridot Fact #1

197

Reader questions for our
Melody kingdom friends!

Q Princess Piano, now I'm curious. What IS the weirdest thing you've autographed?

Don't ask.

Q Queen Cymbal, do you ever perform onstage like your daughter?

WELLL

Don't ask.

Q Piano, how long have you been performing?

The Song Festival is coming up next month, sooo...

10 years.

You can remember that far back?

Well, there's a good reason.

Queen Sapphire was visiting from the Crystal kingdom, and it was a **huge** deal.

We all wanted to impress her, you know?

Welcome!

I rehearsed and rehearsed...

Melody Miscellany

Did you enjoy your time in the Melody Kingdom? Are you itching to learn more about its people, history...and maybe a few things you never wanted to know? Well, itch no more! (And then keep reading.)

Let's start with the royal family! You remember Princess Piano and Queen Cymbal, right?

But...

Wait a second, did **King Clarinet** ever introduce himself?

Dad's a little shy.

You might have noticed that Trebleopolis lacks knights, unlike most other royal cities in Dreamside. But never fear, because Queen Cymbal's elite Clown Squad is here!

...To spread some cheer!

When they aren't keeping the peace in town, they're great for parties.

If you're looking to do some sightseeing, hot-air balloons like the ones shown to the right are popular in Trebleopolis, but...

...Queen Cymbal's pride and joy, the *Ocarina Blimp*, is the fastest way to get over the enormous(ly inconvenient) Intermezzo Wall.

Speaking of which, remember the two kings who divided the country over their tastes in music?

King Treble and King Bass were brothers, and they actually got along pretty well otherwise. It's a good thing they could still visit each other from time to time!

You might have guessed that **Trebleopolis** was named after the ancient King Treble. It has always been as cheery (and loud) as it is today!

There was also a city called **Bassville** back then, located near modern-day Rhythm Ridge. King Bass' palace used to be a dark, gloomy place until Noisemaster made it his own during the Nightmare Knight's first conquest.

After Noisemaster's arrival in Bassville, King Bass and his subjects fled deep into Waltz Woods, where they founded a new village called Organetto.

Shortly thereafter, the king was betrayed by his most trusted court magician, a young man named Legato, who seized control of the town and ruled with a (beautifully manicured) iron fist!

It's said that Legato was so powerful that even the spirits haunting Waltz Woods were bound to his will.

Count Legato was eventually bested by Gherkin, the first legendary hero, on his way to challenge Noise and Mutemaster. At the moment of his defeat, Legato sealed his power into the contact lens we saw in Chapter 2.

Nowadays, we kind of do whatever we want, though.

Keeping that contact lens hidden away for all eternity is definitely the most responsible thing to do, here.

...But if it could turn little Panpipe into "Prince Crescendo," you have to wonder what it might do to other characters...

Princess Piano

Atk ★
Def ★
Sp ★★

🎹 "piano" pendant
💝 fan gifts
✉ red envelope

The Melody Kingdom princess is said to
have Dreamside's loveliest voice...when
she's not screaming her head off.
For some reason, her mind seems to be
elsewhere these days. What could be
troubling her?

Commander Caboodle

Atk ★★★★
Def ★★★★
Sp ★

⚫ justice navi
⛑ justice helmet
🔑 justice ship key

This space-traveling oddball has made
it his mission to defend the defenseless
in the name of **JUSTICE!!** Despite his
over-the-top, uh...**everything**, he
seems like a good guy. But who could
he be looking for?

Noisemaster

Atk	★★★★
Def	★★
Sp	★★★★

- 🎵 mixtape
- 🎧 cool phones
- 👕 zig-zag cape

Ya boy's in the house! Who's ready to make some **NOISE**?! Don't be fooled by his showmanship — this Master's quick, cunning, and serious when it really matters. How did such a little guy build that huge Noise Blaster, anyway?

Mutemaster

Atk	★★★
Def	★★★★
Sp	★★★★★+

- 📄 light reading
- 🎧 gentle earmuffs
- ☕ china collection

The third Disaster Master was created at the same time as Noisemaster, with whom he shares an unbreakable bond. He's usually calm, but once he gets mad, watch out! His Mute Zone power is fearsome, and he's physically tough, too. He'd be unstoppable, if not for...

Concept Art

control room (blue)

Now for the other half!

Better finish up that first one.

Cold stare down, but not angry

almond takes a hit

cucumber/nautilus/carrot all react

almond hits the wall, falls to the floor

mute makes his way over

leaves small mute zones in footprints

creates a mute zone around almond

show it extending around the room

"be careful, cucumber!" (show it creeping up.)

"wait — THAT was —!" he's muted.

Nautilus: "N... No." she's the only one left outside the mute zone.

too official

cloudy trim

day

night

Bonus Story I: Bland Salad

What I wouldn't give to make you look at me the way you look at her...

To hear you speak **my** name with the same longing...

Oh... I could die happy.

Lettuce?

No, not like that.

Lettuce??

Like, huh??????

Uh...are you okay?

You've been spacing out more than usual. I'm getting kinda worried.

You? Worried about **me**? Don't make me laugh.

Well, anyway!

Pat

Less talking, more looking!

Y...

Yeah...

International baking competition?

Very exciting, no?

I am thinking it is a chance to, how you say, "settle the score"...

But it seems that you did not receive a letter.

This is too bad, ah?

What?!

Have we lost that much popularity?!

Oh, how mortifying...!

B-Big **deal**, man! Who wants to enter some fancy-pants contest, anyway?!

Ummmm...

WHAT?!

ohhhh

I-I jusht wanted to shay... Your letter'sh right here.

You shaid you didn't feel like goin' through the mail, so it was jusht lyin' on top of a buncha junk.

Baguette.

W-Whoops! Read that to us, would ya?

"To the Bakerette Sisters,
You are cordially invited to participate in the very first Seafoam City Bake-Off..."

Seafoam City?!

Before our Almond Battle gets under way, a friendly handshake between our competitors.

U-Um...

Uh...

I-It'll be a r-real honor...

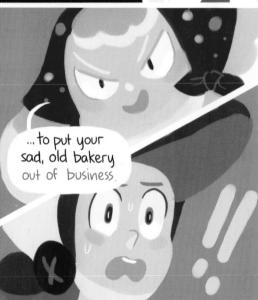
...to put your sad, old bakery out of business.

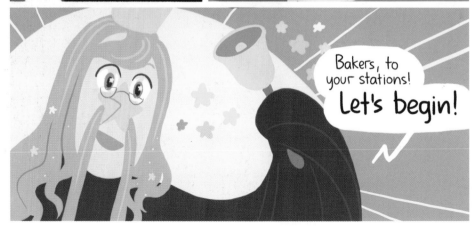
Bakers, to your stations!

Let's begin!

Done!!

So fast!!

And a biased judge, too...

There's no way we can win, hon!

Keep it together, Tartelette! We've still got a chance if we just—

HA HA HA!!

Wow, Almond.

This is rich.

Dear, is this really all right?

Hm... I suppose now **would** be the time for an impassioned speech...

"Our kingdom shall not fall to the likes of you," and so forth...

...but, seeing as our daughter is currently on a quest to defeat you, I think we'll leave the heroics to her.

That would be wise.

Come, Peridewt.

STOOOOOOPP!!

Thank you for reading!

The Melody Kingdom

Intermezzo Wall

Trebleopolis

Pizzicato Park

First Second

New York

Copyright © 2018 by Gigi D.G.

Published by First Second
First Second is an imprint of Roaring Brook Press, a division of
Holtzbrinck Publishing Holdings Limited Partnership
175 Fifth Avenue, New York, NY 10010

Library of Congress Control Number: 2017946148

Hardcover ISBN: 978-1-250-15983-0
Paperback ISBN: 978-1-62672-834-9

Our books may be purchased in bulk for promotional, educational,
or business use. Please contact your local bookseller or the Macmillan
Corporate and Premium Sales Department at (800) 221-7945 ext. 5442
or by e-mail at MacmillanSpecialMarkets@macmillan.com.

First edition, 2018
Book design by Rob Steen

Cucumber Quest is created entirely in Photoshop.

Printed in China by RR Donnelley Asia Printing Solutions Ltd.,
Dongguan City, Guangdong Province

Hardcover: 10 9 8 7 6 5 4 3 2
Paperback: 10 9 8 7 6 5 4 3 2 1